Kitty Kingdom

~ Tabby Takes the Crown ~

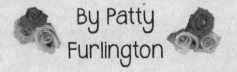

By Patty
Furlington

Scholastic Inc.

Text copyright © 2019 by Working Partners Limited
Cover and interior art copyright © 2019 Scholastic Inc.

All rights reserved. Published by Scholastic Inc., Publishers since 1920, 557 Broadway, New York, NY 10012, by arrangement with Working Partners Limited. Series created by Working Partners Limited, London.

SCHOLASTIC and associated logos are trademarks and/or registered trademarks of Scholastic Inc. KITTEN KINGDOM is a trademark of Working Partners Limited.

ISBN 978-1-338-29237-4

10 9 8 7 6 5 4 3 2 1   19 20 21 22 23

Printed in the U.S.A.   40
First printing 2019
Book design by Baily Crawford

With special thanks to Conrad Mason

To Oscar Wood

Table of Contents

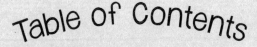

Chapter 1

QUEEN FLUFFYPANTS HERSELF

"There she is!" cried Nanny Mittens. She fanned herself with a paw. "Oh my . . . It's Queen Fluffypants!"

Princess Tabby giggled. "I don't know why she's so excited," she whispered to her brothers, Prince Felix and Prince Leo. "It's only a statue!" All the same, she couldn't help feeling a little bit excited herself.

The town square was full of kitizens

hanging up flags, sweeping the streets, and getting everything ready for the Founding Day Festival. The statue had been put up in the very middle of the square. The three royal kittens stood on tip-paw, trying to see it over the heads of the crowd.

"I can't see a thing!" said Leo. The little orange cat hopped from paw to paw, but he was too small. "When do we get to cut the ribbon and open the festival?"

"Ooh, I hope the scissors aren't too sharp," worried Tabby's older brother Felix. "I don't want to cut myself!"

Tabby's tail flicked with impatience. *I can't wait for it to start*, she thought. There was going to be fluffy pink cotton catnip, a giant Ferris wheel, and every kind of ride. *And we get to open the festival for everyone!*

"Come along," said Nanny Mittens, leading the royal kittens through the crowd. "There, we're nice and close now."

Tabby stared up at the statue. Her parents, King Pouncalot and Queen Elizapet, had ordered it to be made in time for the festival, and it towered over the middle of the square. She felt a shiver of wonder. *It's much more amazing than I expected!*

Queen Fluffypants was made of shining gold, but she looked very stern. She wore her pants tucked into tall boots and had a sword hanging from her belt. Tabby wished she could dress like that all the time. Today

Nanny Mittens had made her put on a fancy silver gown with golden stars on it.

"The Founding Day Festival is held in honor of Queen Fluffypants," Nanny Mittens was saying. "Did you know, she was the—"

"—first ruler of Mewtopia!" interrupted Tabby. She grinned. "You've already told us that, Nanny!"

"Have I really?" Nanny Mittens frowned, then combed Tabby's whiskers with a claw. "How are you three always so messy? This whisker on the left is always so crooked . . ." She turned to smooth the black fur on Felix's head. "And that tuft of yours just won't stay down, will it?"

"Stop fussing, Nanny!" wailed Leo. He squirmed as Nanny Mittens wiped his ears.

"Always so dirty!" said Nanny Mittens. "Now, I'm sure I've never told you about the Three Rules of Queen Fluffypants."

The royal kittens shared a look. *Only a hundred times!* thought Tabby.

"These rules have been passed down to royal cats from the time of Queen Fluffypants," said Nanny Mittens. She cleared her throat. "Listen carefully, please. Rule Number One: *Always—*"

"*Trust your whiskers!*" said Felix, proudly.

"Er . . . very good," said Nanny Mittens. "Rule Number—"

"Two," said Leo. *"Many paws are better than one!"*

"And Rule Number Three," said Tabby as Nanny Mittens opened her mouth. *"In dark times, look for light to guide you."*

"Bless my whiskers!" said Nanny Mittens. "I *am* impressed! Well, since you all know so much about Mewtopian history, how about an art lesson instead?" She brought out three little pads and three pencils from her apron and passed them around. "I thought we could each do a drawing of the statue. Then we can show them to your parents!"

Tabby's ears twitched anxiously. She loved drawing, but right now she would much rather be in their tree house in the palace garden. From up there, they would be able to see the whole festival.

Nanny Mittens yawned. "All this excitement," she purred. "It's making me rather"—*yawn*—"sleepy."

Tabby nudged her brothers. "If we could just get her to take a nap," she whispered, "then maybe we could sneak away!"

Leo winked at Tabby and Felix. Then he patted the stone step leading up to the statue. "Why don't you sit on this nice comfy step, Nanny?" he said.

"You can rest your head on my coat!" added Felix, rolling it up into a bundle.

"I'll give you a paw!" said Tabby, helping Nanny Mittens to sit down.

"Well, that is a tempting offer," said Nanny Mittens. "Leaping fleas, that *is* comfortable! Goodness, I could just"—*yawn*—"fall . . . asleep . . ."

Nanny Mittens's head drooped onto Felix's coat. Her eyes closed. And a moment

later, her whiskers were rising and falling as she snored loudly.

"Great idea, Leo!" whispered Tabby. *Nanny Mittens loves catnaps more than anything!*

"Let's go to the tree house!" said Leo.

Tabby grinned. "Last one there's a wimpy mouse!"

"Then let's come straight back here," said Felix. But the others were already dashing off, their tails waving.

Soon afterward, the royal kittens had climbed up into the tree house.

Captain Edmund had made it from planks of wood, high in the branches of an oak tree. Now they leaned out of the window, watching kitizens in the streets far below. The rides were in the meadow beside the town, and there were lots of kitizens heading there, all in fancy clothes and costumes. They crowded around the gates, waiting for the festival to begin.

"Look at that costume!" said Felix. He pointed at three kittens walking one after the other, each wearing one part of a huge, silvery fish outfit.

"They look yummy!" said Leo, licking his lips. "Hey, those ones are dressed as the Whiskered Wonders!"

The royal kittens peered down at some little kitties gathered around a cotton catnip stall. They all wore black, with colorful scarves tied over their faces.

"They look just like we do in our secret outfits," said Tabby. She grinned. No one in all the kingdom knew that she and her brothers really were the Whiskered Wonders. They had saved the kingdom three times before. But they always wore costumes, so no one would suspect who they really were.

"Imagine if those kitties knew the real Whiskered Wonders were watching them right now!" said Leo.

Felix nibbled his claws. "I have a bad feeling we'll need those outfits again . . .

King Gorgonzola said he'd never stop trying to take over the kingdom!"

The royal kittens fell silent. Tabby knew
they were all thinking about the horrible
rat king, with his greasy black fur, his
ragged cloak, and his spiky iron crown . . .

"Who cares about that stinky rotter?"
said Leo at last.

Tabby frowned. She definitely didn't
want King Gorgonzola to ruin the festival.
But she almost hoped he would try something . . . *Then we could have another adventure,
like Silverpaw!* Silverpaw was Tabby's favorite kitty hero, and she loved hearing about
him in the stories Nanny Mittens read
them at bedtime.

Then the kittens heard a nasty laugh from somewhere close by.

Peering down from the tree house, they spotted three funny-looking figures crouched by the palace walls. They were all wearing kitten ears attached to head-bands. But they weren't cats. Their faces were too thin. Their paws were too pink. And their tails were too long and scaly . . .

Tabby's heart quickened.

"Rats!" Felix gasped.

"Not just any rats," whispered Tabby. "It's Brie!"

"And Chedd," added Leo.

"And Mozz," finished Felix. "King Gorgonzola's sneaky servants!"

"What terrible costumes!" Leo scoffed. "We spotted them in no time."

"Shh!" said Tabby. "Let's listen . . ."

As the royal kittens fell silent, Brie spoke up. "Just wait," she said. "This is his best plan yet!"

"His Revoltingness is so smart," said Chedd. "I can't wait until he steals it!"

"Steals what?" asked Mozz.

Brie rolled her eyes. "Keep up, cheese-for-brains. King Gorgonzola is going to steal the Crown of Mewtopia, remember? And he's going to do it today!"

Chapter 2

THE ROYAL MAZE

"Did you hear that?" hissed Felix as the rats ran off. "The Crown of Mewtopia!"

Tabby's heart was thumping. The crown had once belonged to Queen Fluffypants and it was the most important treasure in the kingdom. Even more valuable than the other items King Gorgonzola had tried to steal.

Leo looked confused. "But he couldn't

steal it even if he wanted to," he said. "Nanny Mittens said so. It's kept right in the middle of the maze in the palace gardens."

"And only royal cats can solve the maze," said Felix.

Still, Tabby couldn't help feeling worried. "What if King Gorgonzola *has* found a way in?" she said. "If he got his claws on that crown . . ."

The royal kittens looked at one another in fear. They were all remembering Nanny Mittens's history lesson about the royal crown. *Whoever wears the crown*, she had told them, *is the ruler of Mewtopia, until someone else puts it on.*

If King Gorgonzola got his paws on the crown and put it on, that would make him ruler of Mewtopia!

"There's only one thing to do," said Leo. "We have to get the crown first—before Gorgonzola can steal it."

"Agreed," said Tabby. "No time to change into our costumes—let's go!"

"I don't like this," said Felix a few moments later, staring up at the maze. It was made out of hedges. They grew like leafy green walls over the royal kittens, stretching out into the distance on either side. Next to the entrance, the hedges were carved into two huge cats, sitting on guard.

Tabby frowned as she looked closer. "Leaping fleas!" She gasped. "There isn't just one entrance . . . There are *three*!"

Sure enough, between the two hedge cats there were three gravel paths leading into the maze.

"Which one do we go down?" Felix worried.

But Leo was already running down the middle path. "Follow me!" he called.

Tabby grinned at Felix. Then she and her older brother darted off after the little orange cat.

The path curved around to the right, but they hadn't gotten far before it forked into two more paths.

"Which one now?" said Leo, frowning at the two paths. "This is tricky!"

"It's *supposed* to be tricky," said Felix. "It's a maze!"

Tabby looked at each path. The one on the left was wide and straight, with low hedges and sunbeams shining down on it. The one on the right was narrow, winding, and dark, with high hedges blocking out the light. "I think we should take the path on the right," she said at last.

Felix started nibbling his claws again. "Doesn't that way look a bit . . . scary?"

"Exactly!" said Tabby. "It's like you said— it's supposed to be tricky. So we won't find the crown by going down the easier path."

Felix sighed. "You're right," he said. "Let's get this over with!"

The royal kittens kept going, following the dark path. It curved left, then right, getting narrower and darker.

Tabby's heart was beating fast. *If there's one thing I really hate, it's darkness!* But she forced herself to keep going.

After a while, they reached another fork.

"Let me guess," said Felix. "We have to go the darker way again, don't we?" There was so little light here that his black fur was completely invisible, and Tabby could only see his green eyes glowing in the shadows.

She swallowed down her fear and agreed.

"What are we waiting for, then?" said Leo.

They came to another fork, then another. Each time they chose the darker path.

"Ouch!" yelped Felix. "That's my tail you're standing on!"

"Sorry," said Leo.

Tabby's fur was sticking up all over as she looked into the blackness. She couldn't see a thing. It was the darkest place she'd ever been in.

"This must be a *magical* darkness," said Felix, his voice trembling.

"And the path's so narrow I can feel the hedges pressing in on both sides," said Leo. "We must have gone the wrong way!"

"We'll be lost in here forever!" wailed Felix.

"No, we won't," said Tabby, trying to be brave. "We just have to think. Remember what Nanny Mittens said? *Only royal cats can solve the maze.*"

"But what do we have that other cats don't?" said Leo.

The royal kittens fell silent, thinking hard. Then Tabby's ears shot up. "I know! We've got the Three Rules of Queen Fluffypants!"

"Passed down from the time of Queen Fluffypants . . ." said Felix. "Maybe the rules are supposed to help us get through the maze!"

"What's the first rule again?" said Leo.

"*Always trust your whiskers!*" said Tabby and Felix, at the same time.

"I think it means we should use our whiskers to feel the way," said Tabby. "If we do that, we can get through the darkness, even if we can't see."

Tabby stepped farther into the maze, and the tips of her whiskers brushed the leaves on both sides. "I think it's working!" she called. "As long as there's space for our whiskers, there's space for us!"

"If you're sure," said Felix doubtfully. But Tabby heard her brothers following along behind her.

She kept going, feeling her way through

the darkness with her whiskers. At last, the maze stopped getting narrower. Her heart was racing, but she felt a little hopeful. *Nanny Mittens's history lessons are finally coming in handy!* she thought.

After a while, Tabby couldn't feel the hedge at all. "I think the path's getting wider again!" she called back.

"It's getting lighter, too!" said Leo.

Sure enough, as they went on, they began to see things through the darkness. They could make out the leaves now, and the gravel beneath their paws. There was even a glimmer of sky, high above.

"Look!" yelled Felix.

Up ahead, the path came to an end at a little wooden door.

Tabby gasped. "Do you think the crown is behind there?"

Leo had already darted on ahead. He twisted the doorknob. He pulled and shoved at the door. But it wouldn't move an inch.

"It's no use!" panted Leo. "I think it's just a dead end."

Felix sighed. "We came all this way for nothing!"

Tabby felt the excitement rush out of her like she was a popped balloon. Then she thought of something. "Maybe it's a magic door, just like the darkness was magical. Hey, do you remember the second rule of Queen Fluffypants?"

"Many paws are better than one," said Felix.

"Exactly!" said Tabby. She twirled her whiskers thoughtfully. "The first rule helped us through the darkness. Maybe we need to use the second rule here." She held up a paw. "The answer must be something to do with our paws . . ."

Leo looked at his own paw in confusion. "I already tried mine," he said.

"But what if we try *all* our paws?" said Felix. "Together!"

The royal kittens looked at one another. Then they joined paws on the doorknob, and together they turned it.

Whooooosh! All of a sudden, the door shimmered and then disappeared completely.

"Whoa!" Leo gasped.

Beyond the door, there was a large square of white marble with hedges on all sides. As the kittens stepped onto it, shadows fell across the marble. Then beams of light began to move around and cut through the darkness.

"I don't like this," said Felix, nibbling his claws again.

"I know," said Tabby. "More darkness!"

Felix shook his head. "I mean, something doesn't feel right. How did Gorgonzola plan to get through the maze? Even if he made it through the darkness, he wouldn't be able to open that door."

Tabby was about to reply, when Leo pounced on a beam of light. "Gotcha!" he shouted. At once, the light moved away. Leo jumped again, swiping with his claws. "Come back here!"

"This is no time for silly games, Leo!" said Felix, rolling his eyes.

Tabby frowned. "I think he might be onto something," she said. "*In dark times, look for light to guide you.* That's the third rule."

"But where's the light coming from?" asked Felix.

Tabby and Felix looked around. The hedges were thick and dark. Then Tabby glanced up. "There!" she cried.

Dangling from a branch, high above the marble square, was a glittering crystal on a string. The light was coming from it, magically beaming in different directions.

"Get it, Leo!" called Felix.

Leo jumped up high, his orange tail waving. His paw closed over the crystal, then he dropped to the marble, landing on all fours. The string went tight.

Suddenly, Tabby heard the sound of rustling leaves. She spun around, and her jaw dropped.

Part of the hedge was swinging open like a door. Behind it stood a white marble stand. And on top of the stand, the royal kittens saw something gold and shiny . . .

"There it is!" cried Leo. He punched the air in triumph. "It's the Crown of Mewtopia!"

Chapter 3

FOOLISH KITTIES

"It's amazing!" Felix gasped.

The royal kittens crowded around the marble stand. The Crown of Mewtopia sat on a blue velvet cushion on top of the stand. It was made of gold, carved with swirling patterns, and decorated with red rubies, each as big as an egg.

"I'm going to try it on!" said Leo, reaching for the crown.

"No!" said Tabby, quickly batting his paws away. "Don't you remember? If you put it on, you become the ruler of Mewtopia! That's why we can't let Gorgonzola get his claws on it."

"I guess you're right," said Leo, sounding a bit disappointed. "Anyway, the crown is safe now. We've beaten that naughty rat again!"

Tabby couldn't help glancing over her shoulder . . . but there was no sign of King Gorgonzola. *That's funny*, she thought. *He hasn't even tried to steal the crown.*

"Let's take it out of the maze," said Felix. "We can give it to Captain Edmund to keep safe."

"Good idea," said Tabby.

Moving slowly and carefully, Tabby took the crown from the cushion. It was lighter than she'd expected, and she felt a flutter of nerves. *What if I drop it?!*

But there was no time to lose. The royal kittens hurried back through the maze. Felix remembered each twist and turn, and this time it was much easier. Every time they turned a corner, Tabby worried they would run straight into King Gorgonzola coming the other way. But they never did.

The paths became wider and lighter, and Tabby felt her heart lift with hope. *We really did it! We rescued the Crown of Mewtopia!* She thought of King Gorgonzola again, but this time she just grinned. *I guess we were too quick for that wicked rat!*

At last, they ran out past the huge sitting cats carved into the hedges at the maze's entrance.

"Phew!" Felix gasped.

"Made it!" said Tabby.

"That was our easiest adventure yet," added Leo, grinning.

And just then, three figures rushed from behind one of the giant hedge cats.

"Stick 'em up! This is a robbery!"

Tabby froze. The three figures were all dressed in black and carrying swords. They had masks tied over their long noses, but she would have known these three any-where. *Besides, they don't have their cat-ear disguises on now.*

"It's Brie," she whispered, "and Chedd and Mozz."

"Give us the crown!" snarled Chedd.

"No way!" shouted Leo.

Tabby held on tightly to the crown. "You're not getting it," she said.

"Oh, aren't we?" said a horribly familiar voice.

The royal kittens whirled around. Just behind the other giant cat stood an old black carriage, with peeling paint and rusty wheels. A greasy rat leaned against it. He had shining yellow eyes, and he wore a long gray cloak and an iron crown. *King Gorgonzola!* He drew a sword and showed his yellow teeth. "Hand over the crown, kitties. Or the nanny gets it!"

He swung open the door of the carriage. The royal kittens gasped.

Lying across the seats was a familiar furry white shape. Nanny Mittens was still gently snoring. *Not even being kidnapped could wake her!* Tabby's heart sank, and her whiskers drooped.

King Gorgonzola laughed. "If you could see your faces! You silly kitties . . . this was all just a trick! I made my servants wear those terrible costumes on purpose. I knew you would rush off to the maze at once and get the crown for me." He twirled his whiskers. "Now I've proved it once and for all . . . I'm much smarter than you fuzzy-faced do-gooders!"

"You're just a smelly ratbag!" shouted Leo.

Gorgonzola snarled. "Is that any way to talk to your future king? Once the crown is mine, I will rule Mewtopia . . . or should I say, Ratopia! You will all bow down to me. And I'll be keeping your nanny, too, just in case you get any silly ideas about trying to stop me." He stepped forward and held out a claw. "Now give me the crown."

The royal kittens looked nervously at one another. Tabby's paws tightened on the crown. *We can't let him become king!* But they

couldn't let him hurt Nanny Mittens, either, even if she did give them too many history lessons.

Tabby's heart sank even further as she realized the truth. *We've got no choice.* She stepped forward and held out the crown.

King Gorgonzola grabbed it, giggling

with excitement. "Mine! Mine! Mine!" he sang. "It's mine! Servants—to the carriage!"

Brie, Chedd, and Mozz darted to the carriage and put on harnesses, ready to pull their king. Then Gorgonzola hopped inside. He gave the royal kittens one last rotten-toothed grin. Then he took off his iron crown and put on the gold one. He slammed the carriage door shut, and at once the rat servants began to pull.

The royal kittens watched, frozen with horror, as the carriage rolled across the gravel and disappeared behind some trees.

Felix was nibbling his claws harder than ever. "What have we done?" he said.

"If we hadn't gone into the maze, he would have never gotten the crown!" wailed Leo.

Tabby felt just as upset as her brothers. *I can't believe we made such a terrible mistake . . .* But she frowned with determination. "We'll have to rescue Nanny Mittens and get that crown back," she said. "Come on! I bet Gorgonzola is heading for the palace."

The royal kittens ran off through the gardens as fast as they could. But when they came out in front of the palace, they stopped suddenly.

Tabby gasped. "What happened?" she said, looking all around.

"I don't believe it!" said Leo.

"Mewtopia," said Felix. "It's . . . gone!"

Chapter 4

WELCOME TO RATOPIA

Everything was completely different.

The flags on the palace walls were black, and instead of the golden claws of Mewtopia, each flag had a chunk of gorgonzola cheese on it. A black banner hung above the drawbridge. WELCOME TO RATOPIA, it said, under a picture of King Gorgonzola's grinning face. HAVE A STINKY STAY!

The royal kittens ducked behind a tree and looked out from behind it.

Whumph! Tabby saw a milk fountain disappear in a flash of light. When she looked again, the milk had stopped and the pool below had hardened into smelly cheese.

Whumph! There was another flash of light. "Look at the yarn factory!" said Felix. The big brick building was now painted yellow, so it looked like a giant piece of cheese. Some sad-looking kitizens in aprons pushed a cart out the front doors, loaded with cheddar. "It's turned into a cheese factory!"

Tabby gazed around in shock. More

kitizens stood at street corners, looking afraid. Even the scratching lampposts had been replaced by wooden chewing blocks. Worst of all, there were rats everywhere. They ran through the streets, shrieking and laughing at the cats.

Suddenly, a trumpet blew. Tabby felt a rush of excitement as she saw a group of cat soldiers charge out of the palace. They all wore shining silver armor and carried swords.

"For Mewtopiaaaa!" they yelled.

They're going to save the day! thought Tabby.

But before they got to the end of the drawbridge—*whumph!*—the cats' armor and weapons disappeared in another flash of light. Tabby blinked. Now the closest rats were wearing the armor instead of the cats.

"How is this happening?" Leo gasped.

"It's the crown," said Tabby. "Its magic is helping Gorgonzola take over the kingdom!" Her heart sank all over again. "Oh, look what we've done. We've ruined everything!"

The rats quickly surrounded the cat soldiers and took them prisoner.

Felix nudged Tabby and Leo. He pointed to the palace's side gate, and Tabby's eyes widened. Captain Edmund had just opened the gate. He checked that no one was looking, then helped two more cats out. *Mom and Dad!* King Pouncalot and

Queen Elizapet were still wearing their royal robes and their normal everyday crowns.

"Phew! At least they're safe," said Leo as Captain Edmund quickly led the royal cats into the gardens.

"We should follow them," said Felix.

Tabby wanted to, but she shook her head. "We can't run away," she said. "This is all our fault!" She felt terrible, but she knew that they had to do something. She thought of her favorite hero, Silverpaw. *In the stories, he rushes straight into danger. But he's smart as well as brave.*

Felix shook his head sadly. "I knew something wasn't right back in the maze."

"We should have listened to you," said Tabby. "Sorry, Felix. We got so excited about having an adventure, we forgot to think it through. It's like Queen Fluffypants said—*always trust your whiskers*. I think she meant more than just using our whiskers in the dark. I think she meant that we should trust our instincts!"

"We'll just have to outsmart Gorgonzola again," said Leo. "Then we'll get Nanny Mittens back. And the crown, too!"

"Come on," said Tabby. "Let's go to our tree house and make a plan."

The royal kittens crept through the gardens, crouching low so that no rats would spot them.

They were just passing by the tallest tower in the palace, when something soft and white came drifting down to land on Felix and cover his head.

"Attack!" yelled Felix, waving his claws about in panic. "I can't see! Help!"

Leo pulled the thing off his brother's face. "It's just one of Tabby's nightgowns!" he said.

The royal kittens looked up. More clothes were falling now. Tabby saw one of her green dresses flying through the air and Leo's favorite red shirt.

"They're coming from our bedroom!" said Leo angrily. "Someone's throwing out all our things!"

Listening hard, the royal kittens heard voices from above.

"Horrible kitty clothes!" cried Brie. "Give me some nice stinky rags any day!"

"And these sheets smell like *perfume!*" Chedd complained. "Let's get rid of them."

"Look at our new bedroom, though!" sang Mozz. "The beds are so soft!"

"They're stealing our room," said Felix sadly.

Just then, another pile of clothes came floating down to land on the grass. "Our costumes!" said Tabby. "Now we can dress as the Whiskered Wonders!"

"I wish we had our swords, too," said

Leo as they pulled the black outfits on over their clothes. "It's going to be hard to fight off the rats without them."

"Don't worry," said Tabby, tying on her mask. "I hid them under the trapdoor in our room so Nanny Mittens wouldn't find them. At least the rats won't, either. Now let's get to the tree house!"

Soon afterward, they had climbed the tree and stood on the platform, staring out the window at the palace. They all had their masks on now. Tabby's was red, Felix's was purple, and Leo's was green.

"Isn't that Nanny Mittens?" asked Felix. Sure enough, they could just see the big white cat through a window in a round tower. She was stretched out on the royal bed, snoring peacefully in the king and queen's bedroom.

"But where's Gorgonzola?" asked Leo.

The royal kittens thought for a moment. "I bet he's in the treasure chamber," said Tabby. "He's always trying to steal our treasures, isn't he?"

"Of course!" said Felix. "He'll probably make it his throne room so he can be close to the treasure all the time!" The black kitten frowned. "But what do we do now? I bet Gorgonzola has lots of guards in there. And he definitely won't want to give us back the crown!"

Tabby nodded. "We need to be smart this time. We have to trust our whiskers! If we can figure out how to get in—"

Just then, they heard a twig snap down below. The royal kittens all ducked down below the window, listening hard.

"I'm sure the drawbridge was here some-where," said a rat's voice.

"This place is like a maze!" grumbled another rat. "Let's try the other way."

The royal kittens waited until they couldn't hear the rats anymore. Then Tabby jumped to her paws. "That's it!" she cried. "*That's* how we get inside! The palace isn't a maze to us. We've been hav-ing adventures in it since we were tiny little kitties. We know ways to get in that they won't know to guard!"

"So can we fight King Gorgonzola now?" asked Leo.

"Not yet," said Tabby. "Huddle up! We're going to make the best plan ever . . ."

Chapter 5

GHOST CATS

Soon after, the royal kittens climbed down the tree and ran to the palace wall. They ducked low. Then they ran to the bottom of the round tower where Nanny Mittens was being held prisoner.

Tabby looked up at the ivy growing against the stones. *I hope it doesn't break*, she thought. Then she flicked her ears to signal to her brothers. One by one, they began to climb.

The ivy grew all the way to the top of the wall. As they passed the window where they had seen Nanny Mittens, Tabby leaned out as far as she could. But the ivy was too far away, and she couldn't reach the window frame.

Felix gently pulled her tail. When she looked down, he whispered. "The chimney!"

Tabby nodded and kept climbing.

The wind blew, rustling the ivy and forcing them to cling on tight. Tabby tried not to think about how high up they were. *One paw at a time . . .*

At last, they reached the top and pulled themselves over. The chimney stood up from the middle of the tower, and together, the three kittens climbed on top of it.

Looking down, Tabby could see nothing but darkness. Her heart raced, but she did her best to ignore the fear. "I'll use my claws to hold on to the sides," she whispered.

"We'll be right behind you," said Leo, his yellow eyes shining with excitement. "*Many paws are better than one*, remember?"

Carefully, Tabby lowered herself into the chimney, holding on to Felix with one paw and Leo with the other. She pushed her claws in between the bricks. Then, slowly, she began to climb down into the chimney.

At last, Tabby saw light from below. There it was! The fireplace leading into her parents' bedroom. As she reached it, Tabby swung herself down and rolled into the room.

A cloud of soot puffed up all around her, and she realized she was filthy. She got to her paws, coughing and dusting herself off. She turned to see Leo and Felix follow, leaving more black paw prints on the carpet.

Leo looked almost as black as Felix did, and Tabby couldn't help grinning. "Look at you, Leo! What would Nanny Mittens say?"

"There's no way she'll recognize us

now!" said Leo. "Not with these costumes *and* the ash."

"Look!" whispered Felix. He pointed, and Tabby turned to see Nanny Mittens still asleep on the red velvet, four-poster bed in the middle of the room.

"Nanny!" cried Tabby. She rushed over and gently shook the old white cat.

Nanny Mittens stirred, yawned, and blinked. She sat up and looked around.

"Are you all right?" asked Leo.

"Oh yes," said Nanny Mittens. "That was a wonderful little catnap. But my whiskers, what am I doing in the royal bedchamber? Who are you nice young kitties? And why are you so dirty?"

Tabby could hardly believe it. *She really had slept through the whole thing!*

"We don't have much time, Nanny," said Felix. "I mean, Ms. Mittens!"

"You've been kidnapped by King Gorgonzola!" said Leo.

"But we're going to get you to safety," promised Tabby.

Nanny Mittens quickly jumped out of bed, her tail twitching with worry. "Leaping fleas! But what about the royal kittens? Are they all right?"

"They're fine," said Tabby. "If you'll just come with us, we'll—"

"Goodness!" said Nanny Mittens suddenly. "I know who you are!" Tabby's heart froze. But then Nanny Mittens grinned. "You're the Whiskered Wonders! What a pleasure to meet you. Of course, I'll do whatever you think is best. Lead the way!"

Phew! Tabby sighed with relief.

Leo lifted up a corner of the carpet and pulled open a trapdoor hidden underneath.

A staircase led down into the darkness below.

Nanny Mittens gasped. "How did you know about the secret passage?"

"Lucky guess!" said Leo quickly.

Tabby couldn't help smiling. She and her brothers had used the trapdoor many times when they were little kitties. Whenever they had a nightmare, they had come here to curl up with Mom and Dad in their bed. The passage led all the way to their bedroom. *And more importantly, to the swords we've got hidden there!* "Come on," she said. "No time to lose!"

Felix led them down the steps. Torches burned in holders on the walls, lighting up the darkness. The passage curved gently around, until finally they reached a dead end.

Leo felt around in the shadows until—*click!*—he found the hidden lever. With a groan, a stone door opened out onto another staircase. Tabby knew that this one led straight up to their bedroom.

"Wait here," Tabby told Nanny Mittens. "We'll be back in no time."

Nanny Mittens nodded and hid in the shadows. Then the royal kittens ran up the stairs to their bedroom.

The door was open just a crack, and Tabby could hear the rats inside.

"I don't want to be a Wimpy Wonder again!" wailed Chedd.

"Tough luck!" said Brie. "That's the way the feta crumbles."

Carefully, Tabby looked around the edge of the door. She saw Brie dressed up in a paper crown, with a black rug over her shoulders. Chedd and Mozz were both wearing their cat ears, and had colored scarves tied around their faces.

"Those are from our dress-up box!" hissed Leo.

"I'm going to get you, Whiskered Weaklings!" growled Brie in a deep voice. "Or my name's not King Gorgonzola!"

"Oh, don't hurt us, Your Rottenness!"

squealed Mozz, hiding under a bed. "We're only silly little kitties!"

"We don't sound like that at all!" snapped Leo.

Felix clapped a paw over Leo's mouth. But it was too late. The rats all froze.

"What was that noise?" said Chedd, scratching his head.

"This place is spooky," said Mozz. His eyes went wide. "Hey, what if there's a ghost?"

"There aren't any ghosts, fur-brain!" snapped Brie. But she still looked around, just in case.

"I hope she's right," whispered Felix, his green eyes wide.

"Of course there aren't any ghosts!" said Tabby. "Unless . . ."

She looked around and spotted a pile of clothes lying outside the door. Tangled among them were the sheets from the royal kittens' beds. *The rats must have thrown them out to put their own smelly blankets on!*

Quickly, Tabby grabbed the sheets and passed them around. Her brothers looked at the sheets. Then, slowly, they both smiled at Tabby.

"Ready?" Tabby whispered when each royal kitten had a sheet over their head. "One . . . Two . . . *Three!*"

Together, the royal kittens ran into the

room, waving their paws and making as much noise as they could.

"Wooooooo!" cried Felix. "I'm a ghoooost!"

"Gooooo awaaaaaay, you ratty rotters!" howled Leo.

"Aaahhhh!" shrieked Brie.

"Ghost cats!" screamed Chedd.

"Run for your lives!" yelled Mozz.

The three rats tore off their costumes and ran. They pushed past the kittens and squeezed out through the door. "Yes!" said Leo, punching the air as the rats disappeared down the staircase.

"Let's get the swords before they come back," said Felix.

In no time at all, the royal kittens had collected the swords from under the trapdoor in their bedroom. They ran down the stairs and found Nanny Mittens. She was still waiting quietly in the shadows.

"What a relief to see you Wonders again!" she said. "I heard the most worrying noises . . ."

"It was only a few ghosts," said Tabby. "Nothing to worry about! Now, to the kitchens!"

This time Tabby led the way, down the steps, through a hallway, and under an arch into the huge palace kitchens.

Normally, this was the busiest place in the whole palace, with pots steaming, cooks shouting, and a fire crackling. But today the kitchens were empty. *It's like this really is a ghost castle*, Tabby thought sadly.

The back door was locked, but Leo and

Felix slid the bolts and pushed it open. Outside were the palace gardens.

"Captain Edmund is out there somewhere," said Tabby.

"With Mom and—" said Leo.

"He means the king and queen!" said Felix quickly. "If you find them, you'll be safe."

"Oh, thank you, my dears," said Nanny Mittens. "But aren't you coming, too?"

Tabby shook her head. "We're going to find King Gorgonzola and steal the Crown of Mewtopia back!"

Nanny Mittens gasped. "Oh my whiskers, that does sound dangerous. But I suppose you *are* the Whiskered Wonders!"

"We just need to find a way into the treasure chamber," said Felix thoughtfully. "I bet there will be guards by the door!"

Nanny Mittens frowned. "The treasure chamber?" She leaned down close and tapped her nose. "If that's where you're going," she whispered, "you'd better go and find Queen Fluffypants first. She will show you the way."

Tabby glanced at her brothers. They looked just as confused as she was. *Queen Fluffypants has been dead for hundreds of years. Has Nanny Mittens lost her marbles?!*

"Good luck!" said Nanny Mittens. She spread her arms wide to sweep them up in a hug. Then she frowned. "That's odd," she said. She reached out and stroked Tabby's face. "A crooked whisker . . ." She turned to Felix. "And that tuft of fur, sticking up like that . . ."

Before Leo could dodge her, Nanny Mittens swept her paw past his ear. "Absolutely filthy!" she said, looking at her paw. "Just like . . . like . . ."

Nanny Mittens gasped. Her eyes went wide. Her fur stood on end. Her tail stuck out straight. "Sweet catnip! You're not just the Whiskered Wonders. You're Tabby! And Felix! And Leo! *You're the royal kittens!*"

The royal kittens froze. Felix looked at Leo. Leo looked at Tabby. None of them knew what to say.

After a long silence, Tabby sighed. "All right!" she said. "It's true. We're the royal kittens!"

"Oh my..." Nanny Mittens fanned herself with a paw. "I feel a little faint..."

"We're sorry we didn't tell you, Nanny," said Felix, looking at the floor.

"But you have to promise not to tell anyone who the Whiskered Wonders are," said Leo. "Especially not Mom and Dad!"

Nanny Mittens was just about to reply, when they all heard pawsteps. They were coming fast toward the door to the kitchens. *Too fast!*

Tabby was sure they only had a few seconds. "Go!" she said. She pushed

Nanny Mittens through the open door, and Felix and Leo slammed it shut.

They had just ducked down under the long kitchen table, when three creatures ran in under the archway. All of them had hairless pink feet and swishing scaly tails . . .

"Uh-oh," whispered Felix. "It's them! It's Mozz, Chedd, and Brie!"

Chapter 6

THE SECRET OF THE LIBRARY

"I told you, I wasn't scared at all!" snapped Brie.

"You said, *Aaahhhh!*" said Chedd.

"I said, *Are!*" said Brie. "I was going to say, *Are you scaredy-rats really frightened of a few ghosts?*"

"I'm not a scaredy-rat!" said Mozz. "I don't even believe in ghosts, so there!"

"Who cares what you believe?" said

Chedd. "I'm going to find a yummy lump of cheese to eat."

Tabby, Felix, and Leo crouched as still as they could as the rats pulled open the cupboards. They threw boxes and cans onto the floor.

"Yuck!" squealed Brie. "Fish sticks . . . sardine sandwiches . . . tuna treats. There's nothing but horrible fish!"

Tabby saw Leo lick his lips. Tuna treats were his favorite thing to eat in all of Mewtopia. Then—*thump!*—an open bag hit the floor, right by the table. Candies went rolling everywhere. They were small and round with gray-and-pink swirls. *Tuna treats!*

"Leo!" Tabby hissed.

But it was too late. Leo dove for the nearest sweet, his paw stretching out to reach it . . . *Clonk!* He hit his head on a table leg. The whole table shook, and Tabby heard plates rattling on top. She froze. *Uh-oh. Now they'll find us for sure!*

"What was that?" screamed Mozz.

"It sounded like . . . *rattling chains!*" wailed Chedd.

"*Ghost* chains!" said Brie.

"Run for your lives!" howled all three rats together. At once, they dropped the cans and boxes they were holding. Then off they ran, out through the archway. Suddenly, the kitchens were silent again.

"Phew!" Tabby sighed.

"They really *are* scaredy-rats!" said Felix as the royal kittens crawled out from under the table. "Even I'm not frightened of ghosts!" But Tabby saw him look around nervously, just in case.

"Are you all right, Leo?" asked Tabby.

Leo rubbed his head. "It's just a little bump. Sorry about that! Those tuna treats are just too tasty." He popped one into his mouth and began to chew as he scooped the rest into his pocket.

"Come on," said Tabby, grinning. "Let's get to the treasure chamber!"

The royal kittens ran off through the halls of the palace.

"Almost there," said Tabby when they were just around the corner from the treasure chamber. "We'd better go quietly . . ."

Felix crept to the corner and peered around the side. "Rats!" he hissed.

"What's wrong?" asked Leo.

"I mean, there are rats there!" said Felix. "They're guarding the door to the treasure chamber."

Tabby groaned. "I knew it! Come on— let's hide in the library while we make a plan."

The royal kittens ran into the library, which was down the next hallway. They ducked down behind one of the huge old shelves full of dusty leather books. There were no rats to be seen. *I bet they don't even like reading!* Tabby thought.

"What now?" asked Leo. "Do we fight the guards?" He drew his sword and swished it through the air.

Felix looked anxious. "I don't know," he said. "It's three against four. And they were all really big!"

"We can't just give up!" said Tabby.

The three kittens fell silent, thinking hard.

"Do you remember that funny thing Nanny Mittens said?" said Felix at last.

"*Go and find Queen Fluffypants first,*" said Tabby. "*She will show you the way.* But Queen Fluffypants is dead."

Leo sighed. "After all those history lessons, I thought I knew everything there was to know about Queen Fluffypants!"

Felix stroked his whiskers thoughtfully. "We *are* in a library," he said. "Maybe we can find a clue in here."

"That's it!" said Tabby. "Let's find a book about Queen Fluffypants!"

The three kittens began looking through the shelves. As Tabby ran her paw along the dusty book covers, Felix gave a shout. "Found one!"

Tabby and Leo ran over to their brother.

He was standing on tip-paws at a book-
case against a wall, trying to reach a thick
red book.

"*The Secret of Queen Fluffypants*," said
Tabby, reading the title on the spine.
"That sounds perfect!"

But as Felix pulled the book out, a rum-
bling sound came from the wall.

"What's that?" asked Tabby, her fur standing on end.

"Uh-oh," said Leo. "Do you think it's rats?"

Then, slowly, the bookshelf was creaking inward. It swung open like a door, and beyond it was a dark corridor.

"Whoa!" said Felix.

"Another secret passage!" gasped Tabby. "I can't believe we never knew about this one!"

"So that's what Nanny Mittens meant," said Felix, putting the book down on the floor. "Queen Fluffypants really *is* going to show us the way. This passage must go straight to the treasure chamber!"

"Good old Nanny Mittens!" said Tabby.

"She's like the fourth Whiskered Wonder!" added Leo.

Quickly, the kittens hurried into the darkness. The passage was narrow, with stone walls and a stone floor. It twisted and turned, and before long it ended at a wooden door.

Tabby slowly turned the door handle, and gently pushed the door open a crack.

Looking out, she saw a big stone room, full of treasure chests. Each one was filled with gold. Torches burned all around, making the metal glow. *The treasure chamber!* Then Tabby saw something that nearly made her jump out of her fur.

Lying on the biggest heap of gold, in the very middle of the chamber, was King Gorgonzola. His cloak was spread over him like a blanket. His mouth was half open. His eyes were closed as he snored. And on top of his head sat something very familiar, made of gold and decorated with large rubies . . .

"There it is!" hissed Leo. "The Crown of Mewtopia!"

Chapter 7

I SMELL KITTIES!

"I don't like this!" whispered Felix. "How do we get the crown without waking him up?"

Tabby looked around the chamber. Just behind King Gorgonzola's head, she saw a smaller heap of treasure. "If we climb on that," she said, "we can reach down and take the crown off his head."

Felix looked very worried. "But which one of us should—"

"Me!" said Leo, hopping up and down. "I'll do it!"

Before anyone could argue, Leo crept out into the room. Tabby and Felix held their breath as the little orange cat crawled slowly, carefully, up the heap of treasure.

As Leo pulled himself higher, Tabby saw the Orb of Plenty glittering among the pile. *The magical treasure that Gorgonzola tried to steal when the royal hounds came to visit!* The orb had the power to multiply food, so the catking and catqueen could feed the whole kingdom. Tabby had seen it make mountains of fish cakes, stacks of catnip creams, and gallons of fresh milk.

At last, Leo reached the top of the pile. Standing on tip-paws, he reached across and slowly lifted the crown from King Gorgonzola's head.

The rat snorted. Tabby gasped. Her heart raced . . .

Then Gorgonzola rolled over and smacked his lips. *He was just snoring!*

Tabby was about to sigh with relief, when Leo spun around and held the crown up. "I did it!" he whispered. "I . . . whoa!"

His paw slipped on a golden mirror.

Crrrrrrrassh!! The whole pile of treasure

wobbled and fell. Leo went tumbling head over tail, tuna treats exploding from his pocket.

The crown went rolling across the floor, and Tabby darted out to scoop it up. Felix grabbed the Orb of Plenty.

Tabby took Leo by the paw. "Let's get out of here," she said. "Quickly, before . . ."

But it was too late. King Gorgonzola sat up. His nose twitched, and his lips curled into a snarl. "I smell kitties!" he roared. His claws flew to his head, and he felt for the crown. He turned, and his yellow eyes landed on the royal kittens. "Thieves!" he screamed. "Guards, arrest them at once!"

Tabby dragged Leo away, but the door to
the secret passage had swung shut. "Sweet
catnip!" She gasped. There was nothing
but a blank wall in front of them.

"There's only one way," said Leo, drawing his sword. "We'll have to fight!"

THUMP! The heavy main door to the

treasure chamber swung open. Four large rat guards ran in, waving their swords. Tabby felt a flutter of fear. *Felix was right*, she thought. *They really are big!* These rats made Chedd, Mozz, and Brie look like tiny little mouse pups.

But Leo didn't seem scared. "For Mewtopia!" he yelled, charging at the rats.

Tabby ran after him. She swung her sword at a big black rat. *Clang!* The clash of steel rang through the chamber. Tabby swung again, and the guard dodged.

The room filled with the sounds of sword fighting. "Get them!" roared King Gorgonzola. "Whiskered Wimps! Take them to the dungeons!"

The black rat stabbed his sword, and Tabby had to duck behind a treasure chest. Looking up, she saw Felix and Leo both fighting hard. Felix still had the orb held tightly in one paw. But slowly, the rats were pushing them back. *They're just too strong for us!*

Their only hope was to get to the door. But there was no way past the guards . . .

The black rat kicked the treasure chest so hard it flew across the floor. Tabby had to roll to one side, and she almost dropped the crown. The guard charged, and she dodged again. *Whoa!* She slipped on something, but she used her tail to balance herself.

Looking down, she saw a little gray-and-pink candy on the flagstones. *A tuna treat!* It must have dropped out of Leo's pocket when he fell.

And suddenly, Tabby had an idea.

"Felix!" she called.

As her brother turned, Tabby kicked the tuna treat across the floor. It stopped just by Felix's paws. For a moment, he looked confused. Then a smile spread over his face.

Felix put one paw on top of the candy and held up the Orb of Plenty. He frowned as he remembered the words of the spell. *"Orb of Plenty, hear my call,"* he said. *"Show your magic, feed us all!"*

At once, the orb glowed with an icy blue light. Then gasps rose up from the rats. Tuna treats were bursting from beneath Felix's paw, sliding across the floor.

"Get him!" screeched King Gorgonzola. "Bring me that orb!"

The rats all rushed toward Felix. But their clumsy pink feet slipped on the rolling candies.

"Whoa!" yelled one as he smashed into a heap of gold coins.

"Uh-oh!" shouted a second. He fell into a suit of golden armor, nose first.

"Yikes!" called the third and fourth rats. They bumped into each other and fell down with a *thump* on the floor.

"Let's get out of here!" said Leo.

Felix and Leo set off, tails waving as they dodged between the guards and out of the treasure chamber.

Tabby followed. She ran as fast as she could. But as she passed King Gorgonzola, she felt a sharp pain in her tail. *Ouch!* She was suddenly tugged backward.

She turned, and her heart sped up with fear. King Gorgonzola had grabbed hold of her tail. And now he was pulling her toward him . . .

Chapter 8

CLAWS UP

"Come here, little kitty," snarled King Gorgonzola.

Tabby struggled, but the rat king just pulled her closer, laughing.

Don't panic ... think! Tabby told herself. She tried to stay calm. There had to be a way out. She thought about how they had gotten through the maze and broken into the treasure chamber. *What would Queen Fluffypants do?*

And all of a sudden, it came to her. *In dark times, look for light to guide you . . .*

Quickly, Tabby lifted the blade of her sword. It shone like a mirror, reflecting the light of the torches around the treasure chamber.

King Gorgonzola almost had her. Any moment now, he would reach out with his horrible claws . . .

Looking over her shoulder, Tabby moved the blade until the reflection of the torch-light shone straight into his face. She felt the rat's grip loosening on her tail. He squeezed his eyes shut, snarling. "Stop that!"

But Tabby just twisted the blade more. The golden light hit Gorgonzola right in the eyes.

"Yaaaaaargh!" At last, the rat let go, flinging his claws up over his eye.

The moment Tabby's tail was free, she ran straight out the door, her heart leaping with relief.

"There she is!" yelled Leo. He and Felix were waiting farther up the hall.

"We were just about to come back for you," said Felix.

"Forget about that!" Tabby held up the

crown. "Let's get this to Mom and Dad before those rats catch us!"

They could already hear Gorgonzola howling inside the treasure chamber. "Get up, you useless ratbags. After them!"

The royal kittens darted through the palace, back into the kitchens, and out to the gardens.

"Stop!" shouted a familiar voice as they ran outside. *It's Brie!* Tabby saw her come rushing around the side of the palace, with Chedd and Mozz not far behind. They were all waving swords.

Felix quickly pushed a statue over, making the rats jump back. The royal kittens ran on, past the rose gardens, across the lawn, and over the bridge.

"King Pouncalot!" yelled Leo. "Queen Elizapet! It's the Whiskered Wonders! We have the crown! Where are you?"

"They must be hiding here somewhere," said Felix, panting hard.

Tabby looked over her shoulder. The rat servants were catching up to them now. Then she spotted King Gorgonzola himself, his gray cloak flying behind him as he joined the chase. "There they are!" he yelled as he led his guards over the bridge. "Don't let them get away!"

"King Pouncalot!" Tabby shouted.

"Leaping fleas!" said a voice.

The royal kittens all spun around. Looking over a garden hedge was Queen Elizapet, her eyes wide with surprise. "It's the Whiskered Wonders!"

King Pouncalot's head popped up beside her. "And they've got the Crown of Mewtopia!"

They must have been hiding behind that hedge all this time! thought Tabby. Her heart leaped seeing her parents again. But she knew they didn't have long. *Any moment now, the rats are going to get us . . .*

"Catch!" called Tabby. She threw the crown over the hedge. King Pouncalot caught it in one paw.

"That's *my* crown!" Gorgonzola snarled.

His rats arrived, forming a circle around the royal kittens.

"Not anymore," said Queen Elizapet. "Your time as king is up!"

King Pouncalot carefully placed the crown on his head. At once, it began to glow with a golden light. Then there were swirls of golden sparks all around them.

Whumph! The rats gasped as their weapons vanished.

"Noooo!" howled Gorgonzola.

Tabby looked back at the palace, and her tail flicked with joy. *Whumph!* Every single black flag turned red. Instead of a stinky cheese, they all had the golden claws of Mewtopia on them again.

"Claws up!" shouted someone. "In the name of Mewtopia!"

Tabby turned and saw Captain Edmund come running from behind the hedge. He had several cat guards with him, all holding bright silver swords.

"Eeeek!" cried Brie.

"Mommy!" wailed Chedd.

"We surrender!" yelled Mozz.

The rats stuck their claws in the air. All except King Gorgonzola. Quickly, he began to run. But as he darted past, Tabby stuck her tail out. *Thump!* Gorgonzola tripped on her tail and fell flat on his nose.

"Curses!" he squeaked. Before he could

wiggle away, Captain Edmund pounced. He held the rat king down on the grass.

Leo punched the air. "Got him!"

"Nice work!" added Felix.

Tabby grinned. *We did it*, she thought. *Mewtopia is saved!*

King Pouncalot and Queen Elizapet stepped out from behind the hedge, holding paws.

"Take this naughty rat to the dungeon at once," said King Pouncalot.

"And his servants," added Queen Elizapet. "They need to have a long, hard think about what they've done."

"Have mercy!" begged Brie.

"We only did it for the cheese!" said Mozz.

"Don't lock me up with these two," said Chedd. "They're more stinky than a rotten Stilton!"

But the cat guards grabbed hold of them and marched them off toward the palace, together with the other rats. Last of all, Captain Edmund pulled Gorgonzola to his claws, holding on tightly to the rat king's cloak.

Gorgonzola scowled at the royal kittens. "This is all your fault," he hissed. "You Whimpering Weasels! You haven't seen the last of me . . . Just you wait!"

Tabby felt a shiver run down her tail as she gazed into Gorgonzola's angry yellow eyes. Then Captain Edmund gave the rat king a push, and he turned away. *Even King Gorgonzola won't be able to escape from the palace dungeon,* thought Tabby. *I hope . . .*

"Whiskered Wonders," said Queen Elizapet. "How can we ever thank you?"

"You've saved the kingdom," said King Pouncalot. "Again!" Then he frowned. "But have you seen the royal kittens anywhere?"

Just then, Tabby noticed a familiar figure walking around the side of the hedge. It was a big white cat, wearing an apron.

"Oh dear, have those naughty rats been captured now?" said Nanny Mittens.

Then she spotted the royal kittens. She stood still. Her eyes grew wide.

Tabby looked at Felix and Leo, and they looked back at her. Her heart was beating faster than ever. *This is it*, she thought. *Nanny Mittens is going to tell Mom and Dad who we really are!* Tabby was sure that their parents would never let them have another adventure ever again.

It's the end of the Whiskered Wonders . . .

Chapter 9

KITTEN KINGDOM

"Yes, Your Meowjesty," said Nanny Mittens, staring straight at Tabby. "I know *exactly* where the royal kittens are."

Tabby closed her eyes. *It's all over! Back to frilly dresses...Back to boring lessons all day long...Back to bowing and curtsying and being well-behaved...*

"Thank goodness!" said King Pouncalot. "And where is that?"

"Well . . ." said Nanny Mittens. "As a matter of fact, they're safe in the palace."

Tabby gasped. She opened her eyes, just in time to see Nanny Mittens give her a wink. "Yes, they are all right," Nanny Mittens went on. "I left them hiding in a cupboard in the kitchens."

"What a relief!" said Queen Elizapet, wiping her forehead. "I'll go and fetch them at once."

"No!" squeaked Felix. His voice shook, and Tabby saw that his fur was all puffed up.

"It's all right, Your Meowjesty," said Tabby quickly. "We can do it."

Queen Elizapet gave a confused smile. "Very well," she said.

"Thank you, Nanny Mittens!" said Leo. He wrapped his paws around the big white cat's leg.

"He means for finding the royal kittens!" said Tabby, pulling Leo away. But just before they ran off, she gave Nanny Mittens a secret wink.

Soon afterward, the royal carriage was on its way to the meadow where the Founding Day Festival would be held.

Tabby and her brothers had quickly changed out of their costumes and hidden them safely in their room. Now, in the carriage, they had just finished telling their parents how they had gone through the maze to find the Crown of Mewtopia.

"Well, that explains how Gorgonzola got his claws on the crown!" said King Pouncalot. "Only royal cats can make it through the maze, you know."

"Sorry, Dad," said Felix.

"We just wanted to help protect the kingdom," added Tabby.

"Like the Whiskered Wonders!" said Leo. His whiskers shook as he tried not to giggle, but luckily the catking and catqueen didn't notice.

Queen Elizapet smiled. "Well, we forgive you," she said.

"And that wicked rat won't be bothering us again," said King Pouncalot. "Thanks to the Whiskered Wonders!"

"Aren't they amazing?" said Felix, grinning.

Captain Edmund was sitting beside the royal kittens. "You know," he said, "I'm not sure we'll ever find out who those Wonders really are."

"Maybe not," said Tabby, trying not to smile. "I just hope we'll get to meet them one day."

Then the carriage stopped. Captain

Edmund swung the door open, and the catking and catqueen stepped down, followed by the royal kittens. A huge crowd of kitizens stood outside, cheering and clapping. "Long live the royal cats!" they called. "Hooray for Mewtopia!"

Tabby saw that the gate into the meadow was open, and a big red ribbon stretched across the gap. In the field beyond she could see the rides, all different colors, glowing in the sunshine. She grinned. *I can't wait!*

Captain Edmund brought a large golden pair of scissors out from the carriage. He passed them to the king and queen, and the royal kittens helped carry them over to the ribbon. Then all five royal cats held the handles carefully.

"All together now," whispered King Pouncalot. "One . . . Two . . . *Three!*"

Snip!

As the scissors closed, the ribbon fell in two, and the crowd cheered even louder.

"Welcome to the Founding Day Festival!" cried Queen Elizapet. "Enjoy yourselves!"

Tabby, Felix, and Leo joined the kitizens streaming into the meadow.

"What should we go on first?" wondered Felix.

"The Ferris wheel!" Tabby and Leo said together.

The royal kittens ran over to the ride and climbed into one of the little carts.

The Ferris wheel began to turn, creaking gently as it carried the royal kittens up into the air. Tabby watched the fairground getting farther away, and she purred with excitement. Kittens ran around on the grass, smiling and laughing. They chased one another in and out of the crowds, past the brightly colored rides, among little stalls selling every kind of treat Tabby could imagine.

"There's Nanny Mittens!" said Leo, pointing. The old white cat was sitting on a blanket in the shade eating a cake with some friends.

"And there's Captain Edmund over by the games," added Felix. "I think he's trying to win one of those fish-shaped balloons!"

As they climbed higher and higher into the blue sky, Tabby sighed. *I've never felt so happy in my life!* She could see all of

Mewtopia now—the towering palace, the shining river, and the rolling green hills beyond . . .

It's our kingdom, she thought. *And it's finally safe!*

Princess Tabby
is no scaredy-cat!

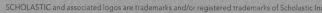